MW01591294

An Alchemy in the Bones

An Alchemy in the Bones

poems

William Reichard

Minnesota Voices Project Number 90
New Rivers Press 1999

© 1999 by William Reichard. All rights reserved
First Edition
Library of Congress Card Catalog Number: 97-69843
ISBN: 0-89823-194-9
Edited by C. W. Truesdale
Cover photograph by Susan Page
Book design and typesetting by Percolator
Printed in Canada

New Rivers Press is a nonprofit literary press dedicated to publishing
the very best emerging writers in our region, nation, and world.

The publication of *An Alchemy in the Bones* has been made possible
by generous grants from the Jerome Foundation; the North Dakota
Council on the Arts; and Dayton Hudson Foundation on behalf of
Dayton's, Mervyn's California, and Target Stores.

Additional support has been provided by the General Mills Foundation,
the McKnight Foundation, the Star Tribune Foundation, and the
contributing members of New Rivers Press.

Excerpt from *Voyage in the Dark* by Jean Rhys copyright 1968 by Jean
Rhys, reprinted by permission of W. W. Norton & Company, Inc.

 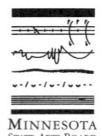 

New Rivers Press
420 North Fifth Street
Minneapolis, MN 55401

www.mtn.org/newrivpr

for my mother

Acknowledgments

The poems listed here, some in slightly different forms, have appeared or are forthcoming in the following publications:

"Three Scenes from the Life of Victor, Wild Child of Aveyron" *Quarter After Eight*

"Song for Frank O'Hara" *Chiron Review*

"Bonsai" *Reclaiming the Heartland: Lesbian and Gay Male Voices from the Midwest; Visions-International*

"The Monster's Dream" *Liberty Hill Poetry Review*

"The Cloud Game" *Chelsea*

"Nijinsky in Love" *Architrave*

"Without Translation" *The James White Review*

"Chromatism: Brown" *Third Coast*

"For a Nun Seeking Refuge in the Form of a Bird" *Chachalaca Poetry Review*

"A Measure" *Spoon River Poetry Review*

"For Liam, When He Grows Up" *Reclaiming the Heartland: Lesbian and Gay Male Voices from the Midwest*

"Autumn Variations" *Folio*

"An Alchemy in the Bones" *Old Crow Review*

"Savoring Mangoes" *Amethyst*

"Mnemonic" *modern words*

"Notes for a Sacred Music" *Art and Understanding*

"Cost of Living" *Chiron Review*

"This Is a Test. This Is Only a Test." *Cimarron Review*

"Constellations" *New Digressions*

"Quiet" *Wolf Head Quarterly*

"It Takes Me" *The James White Review*

"Now That We Are Never Finished Mourning" *Chelsea*

"There Be Monsters Here" *Evergreen Chronicles*

"The Window, Autumn" *Georgia Review*

"Lobelia" *Folio*

"Jerry Lee Lewis Kills His Child Bride" *Queerly Classed: Gay Men and Lesbians Write about Class*

"Fort Collins, Colorado" *Bellowing Ark*

"A House Over There" *Raven Chronicles*

"He Will Not Eat Rice" *The Denny Poems 1993–1994; Outerbridge*

"Diane" *Poets On: Coping*

"My Mother Visits the Site of the Fire" *Mockingbird*

"Notes for a History of Someone Else's Grandmother" *Spoon River Poetry Review*

"My Father Speaks" *1995/96 Anthology of Magazine Verse & Yearbook of American Poetry; Spoon River Poetry Review*

"Three Funeral Songs for Linda" *Connecticut Poetry Review*

"Time Lapse" *Reclaiming the Heartland: Lesbian and Gay Male Voices from the Midwest*

"Unearthed" *Sidewalks*

The author wishes to thank Michael Dennis Browne, Patricia Hampl, Natalie Reciputi, and John Engman, as well as the Jerome Foundation, the Minnesota State Arts Board, and the Headlands Center for the Arts.

Contents

One

Two

One

An Alphabet

The branch, blanketed in ice, finishes in brittleness
and twigs scatter in the snow, form ideograms;

how many words are there for cold? for hunger?
The wind is steep, strips every street clean of traffic,

the possibility of travel. I learn two more words.
The ice recalls an impression of every foot,

retains the pattern of weight, the measure
of each of us. This is a science of retention;

what the elements keep, what the body records
of others. My arms are a slate upon

which your fingers have written; I touch them
when you are not here, read the letters

you have inscribed, hear your absent words
repeated as I pillow out into the snow.

Three Scenes from the Life of Victor, Wild Child of Aveyron

I.
He is pulled from the trees and given a hair brush;
he beats it against his bare legs until symmetrical patterns of blood
bloom up and down his thighs. He is unable to speak.

For his debut: a suit of deep olive green,
a tie which remembers the summer, brown shoes.
He walks into the trees and disappears.

Only his voice remains, the light howling, the wind's voice,
the voice of the leaves. For his debut: a suit in sympathy
with the branches, a grass suit to match his eyes.

II.
Fork. Fork. Plate. Knife. Spoon. The smallest spoon
scrapes out the marrow. He recognizes marrow but
cannot suck the bones now like bloody stalks of cane.

The food is all soft. The flavor of the earth
is washed into the tub with his hair;
everything is pulled back tight.

The right fork makes the difference between derision and pleasure.
Pleasure sits pierced on the tines of a silver fork, propped on the edge
of a butter knife. He is unable to speak, but nods and bows,

has dreams about severed limbs jumping on the ground:
hand and handless arm, foot, footless leg.
He is told to put them back together.

III.
Every time he passes the forest he cowers, remembers in flashes
too fast for the verbal. He is able to speak but never tells anyone
the names of the trees, the names the trees call themselves.

There is always polite conversation. Strings tie his clothes
closer to a body that longs for grass and mud.
He wears a hat with a brim that masks the stars.

Everyone asks if he is hungry. He nods and accepts
the gifts they present. There is a virtue in saying yes.
No one asks about the trees.

Song for Frank O'Hara

The summer's over. I know this because today I finished reading a biography
of Frank O'Hara that I started in June and now it's September; the sumacs
are burning red with that autumn urgency. Some days, I don't know how
to be a poet. A paperboy goes by with his paper bag, its orange strap handle
wound around his chest. He's not a boy
>   *really*

because I want him and I follow him
>   *with my eyes*

down the street; he's safe, though, because I am here in my sunporch, on
my sunchair whose seat has grown to fit my wide, tired ass, and he's safe
because I am too tired to rise and I am too timid.

>   *Oh what pleasures I eat in my dreams! What painful, ecstatic joys!*

I've always tried to like Frank O'Hara's poetry. I've taught "Ave Maria" to
puzzled kids who've never had sex in a dark theater and only one girl
ever got the irony of Frank O'Hara being run down by a dune buggy on
a Fire Island beach.

>   *What do the Muses do when a poet gets a ruptured liver?*

I've never much succeeded in understanding Frank O'Hara. And maybe
that's not the point; I don't always know what poetry is for, how to weave
today's humid weather and the TV shows I saw last night into a good, dense
tapestry. Today I'm sitting in a chair and Frank O'Hara hovers over me.

>   *I'm so sick of angels in these desperate years that I won't give him*

wings—he's just
>   *hovering*

>   *like a nice, horny balloon you see in a*

Macy's parade, but with an erection in one hand and a pen in the other—
somebody get that man a drink!

6

I'm making sense of the small things: The mouse traps Troy set last night that won't spring because mice hate peanut butter, the smell of Josh's hands on my collar, and a persistent, nagging feeling that I'm leaving someone out. Hello to the boy in black who just passed by my window! I think he had dark hair.

I'll later claim he did.

Hello to Frank O'Hara! It's very hot today and the state of my art is beyond recognition; I think I see a poem in here somewhere.

Bonsai

for Troy Linck

We know what is left after roots have been cut
clean away, what remains after limbs have been pruned,

dwarfed by the lips of our sweet scissors,
the blades of our small knives.

And we have constructed ourselves in this same manner,
trimming back families and familiars to base essentials,

pruning back all that we've come from to all that we desire.
We have constructed our lives along the lines of the reductive,

waiting after every stinging cut to see if we can live
without that particular branch, that puny limb.

It's about what can be bent; branches cowed into curvature,
aesthetics dictating nature, and you and I watching

those square porcelain pots for a day or a decade
and maybe nothing will change, maybe one new leaf

in the space of eighty years, one new shoot.
And yet, we wait, learning slowly the distance

through which we can push ourselves,
the subtle growth of trees.

The Monster's Dream

Remarkable that the skin has such resiliency,
that the mechanics of tendon and bone
bend to this extent.
Where is the magic of breath?
On winter mornings, I've watched people
breathe, and their breath pours
from their mouths in a solid cloud;
these people wake the air, the heavens
issue out of them in white vapors.
Once, a man was dipping water from a pool.
I crept behind him and looked
over his golden shoulder;
it was the symmetry that startled me,
the color of his eyes, blue
as if the sky had nested inside.
When my face rested in his
on the silver surface of the water,
the way it only can in water, he screamed.
I had never stood so close to a man before.
What I remember now is the way his mouth
moved as he spoke, the scent of his breath
like sweet fruit and soil, the surface of the pond
as our twin faces shattered,
the way his blue eyes spread out and out
as the ripples sought the farther shore.

Arrangement, with Moon

I sit with Troy and rearrange the furniture at night.
We don't actually move things, but talk about moving things,

talk about moving. God created the world in the dark,
set the little animals down one by one until the planet

was populated enough to sustain light.
We do not turn on the lights as we discuss our plans.

We let the darkness fill instead the blueprints of
our new arrangement. This chair here. That picture there.

That picture out. We've been trying this now
for twelve years and everything is still in process.

Some planets are never complete.
A probe has reached Jupiter, for instance,

and sends back photos of red gas and storms
which have raged for over three centuries.

No light there. No pairs of little animals
nor the rib of man to set things in

some self-conscious, calculated order.
We decide that our apartment has become filled

and thus, is finished. We didn't plan this order.
We never calculated anything.

At 1:00 A.M. Troy says he has to sleep
and walks from dark dining room

to dark bedroom and closes the door.
Outside the window, the watery moon

is silver and insistent. I wonder how much longer
we will live together. I have never seen such light.

The Cloud Game

The clouds carry in another of June's remonstrances. Last week
the wind blew so hard a single strand of straw was driven
through a window without breaking the glass. We take

our meanings where we find them: eyes in the sky; the face of God
in the clouds; the visage of Christ in a hand towel or the bark
of a tree. On the hill, in Medjugorje, where the sun dances

and the Virgin speaks, not one rock or pebble remains.
Pilgrims have carried them off, hoping to be healed or at least
reminded of faith. When I was ten, the sky turned gray, then green,

and the wind screamed in the trees. When I emerged
from the basement, I found an apple tree sitting in a garden
where none grew. In those few minutes under the stairs,

I prayed, and God or something spared the house that is today
fallen into ruin. Perhaps I didn't pray hard enough, and only delayed,
but not denied, that final destruction. In the ceiling of the room

where I grew from child to man, I play the cloud game, searching
in the water stains that daily grow for some report from heaven,
a face in the plaster which comforts as it collapses, a guarantee

for anyone under that roof that she or he will sleep safe,
that the worst of what the heavens offer will be stayed,
the sternest of salvation's sky spared them.

Nijinsky in Love

His body, muscle-hard, bent like a plank
over the plump mound of Diaghilev's belly,

forms a counterpoint. Now, he believes balancing
is the best any dancer can do. His taut lines

as he moves across the stage will not be measured:
the specter of the Rose, the delicate copulation

of the Faun. A crowd hisses and he kisses
Serge's lips once, behind the curtain.

In the balcony, in the wings, in the bedroom,
everyone watches; there is always performance.

Curled in Diaghilev's thick arms,
he dreams of St. Petersburg, of dancing flat

the Rites of Spring, two dimensions come to life.
He dreams of his brother, the way that madness,

like water, seeps into currentless days.
There has never been anything but Diaghilev,

and dance, even in sleep.
He watches the rising, the sinking of Serge's chest.

It will not last, all of this fluid movement,
this quiet rest. Love, like dreams,

like bodies and tides, recedes; it is inevitable,
this split, this new lack of dreaming.

13

Slow Meditation

The rock, white with guano where the pelicans nest,
looked like a pale ship caught in low tide.

The summer's shore gave up nothing but
some broken sand dollars and starfish, clinging

colorless and living in the tide pools at the base of the rocks
the locals called the Three Sisters. As in Chekhov,

they whispered secrets, and their waiting was painful.
That summer, someone had been shooting seals.

Oily black messengers of the sea, swimming
just close enough to the surfers to be mistaken

for those young men in slick black suits on their boards,
each black head bobbing in the cresting and receding waves.

No one knew who was killing them, or why.
Some said fishermen, angry and tired of sharing their catch.

Some said thrill-seeking teens, looking for that lasting surge
in a world devoid of the need for hunting.

Some said the surfers themselves, tired of those pointed faces
staring back at them like mirrors in the frigid water.

I was living in the Headlands then, in a valley cupped
by barren hills, an echo chamber for the sea and the animals

in recovery at the Marine Mammal Research Center,
one valley away. At night, I went to sleep to the cries

of seals and otter, eucalyptus creaking, my house
surrounded by a grove of those trees which

the Indigenous Plant Society members threatened
to eradicate in the name of floral purity. Walking on the beach

on the day of the Daisy Eradication—the Society's members
swarming the hills with black bags and trowels, uprooting

the unwanted immigrants from their foothold in the foothills—
I found a murdered seal. He was lying quietly, sleeping to

my untrained eyes, but frightening, sleek, sand crusting
his tender belly. Yet, not breathing. The stench was enormous,

and between his two closed eyes was a third, open orifice,
jagged, irregular, bloody but dried now, massing with flies,

the hole where his life had looked out at the sea, then fled,
leaving a swelling, dead carcass behind. The gulls circled

cautiously. On the bluff above, a vulture sat and waited for me
to leave and I wondered: Is all life based on such economy?

Living and dying, feasting and starving? I stood on that beach
with the need that had carried me to California, the hunger

for sun in a city blanketed by fog, the will to leave
the constant threat of winter's sleep. And still, I was unfed,

and even the birds knew more about finding what they needed
than me, a landlocked boy who had grown up away from the water,

who couldn't recognize death, who had never even learned to swim.

Without Translation

With sewn lips he speaks
    in a dazzling code that I cannot translate.

But the body has other mouths from which to speak,
    and these, I do comprehend:

How the blade of the shoulder has a tongue,
    and speaks.

How the abdomen, sweetly heaving, has a tongue,
    and speaks.

And the legs stretching, twining, have their language of muscle,
    and speak.

I wish I had a key, the proper code to unlock
    the door to his desire,

a dictionary to decipher the distance
    which my mind cannot span,

but my dry heart, my lips, my clumsy instinct,
    can.

Chromatism: Brown

In the country, in my mother's town,
flags are the new thing. Flying from the tops
of garages, the fronts of porches;
prefabricated family coats of arms
collected from cartoons with
your own special message to the world:
Hello! from Minnie. Hello! from Mickey.
Hello! from the cat with one paw raised
in recognition of the Buddha.
Hello! from the Buddha.
In November, everything is browned down
to one infinite shade. It's the cloudiest month.
I sit at the window in my mother's house
and look out at the street I grew up on.
A brown car passes. Someone has cut down
some trees I remember. Someone else
has placed a ring of stones around their yard,
encircling their house like a plain, brown temple.
In the kitchen, the turkey is browning
and my mother and sisters are blowing smoke
from their clouded lungs. My mother coughs
and it's a wet sound, brown, round, drowning.

From the peak of her garage her flag is flying.
Maybe our family coat of arms, though no one
has ever explained the symbolism to me:
A cat, a dog, a horse, a cow, all smiling,
marching en masse on a field of red and blue,
the word *Welcome* supporting them.
The color of the flag is startling, red against
a sky that, though blue, looks brown.
It's like a cardinal sighted in winter,
just outside your window: red against
that unforgiving field of white—
crimson, vivid, shining.

For a Nun Seeking Refuge in the Form of a Bird

She stands thin and brown
in the green water,

waiting as if waiting
might carry some semblance

of reward. The estuary,
cut off from the sea,

carries its own rhythm.
A fish swims by. Her head

darts beneath the tide
and she is fed

with determination,
the metallic flash of scales.

This may last for hours,
but she has learned nothing

if not patience, sweet,
gentle guile. At dusk,

she gathers her feathered
habit about her, goes

hunting in the reeds
for her little boat,

a refuge from darkness.
Flight is not what

she thought it
would be, the pain

in the shoulders,
the endlessness of

salvation's sky.
A foghorn sounds.

Vespers. She closes
her eyes to desire,

but never to the knowledge
of wanting. Leda, she recalls,

married her swan
in a shower of golden

light. As she has married
her own form, her heart

now caged by the hollow ribs
of a bird, her own body

in flight, seeking always
the further horizon,

the arms of her
skybound lover.

Pomegranate

for Elizabeth Mische

Even the girl-child knew how to eat the fruit,
but the man winced when the woman
stuck the knife in, probed the thick slit
with fingers which emerged
crimson and bloody.
Confident in her act of trespass,
she pried the lips of the skin
apart and pulled; the two halves
split roughly and fell into the plate,
exposing each red nodule,
the white flesh nesting the ripe seeds.
She plucked a seed and ate it.
The girl-child followed suit.
But the man hesitated, staring
at her red fingers, the way
her flat lips were blooming
crimson as she chewed.
One seed, that's what he took
between his fingers, and it
was not so soft as he'd imagined,
more like a kernel or a pellet.
When he bit, there was only
subtle flavor, some juice,
the taste of anticipation
and something more ancient.
Then, just the sensation
of grit, of a seed ground apart.
The woman and her daughter
saw the expression on his face,

23

the way his eyes searched
for some place to quietly spit.
The woman took another seed
and popped it into her mouth,
chewed and grinned, her teeth
stained red. She shook her head
and smiled and said
Persephone did it. Just like this.
Ate and swallowed.
Swallowed the whole thing.

Rodeo Beach, California
Creation

At night, there is no delineation, only gradations
of gray and black, rhythm and sea.
Waves draw an aural measure between
blind land, blind water, bend rocks back to recede,
subtly, with each tide. There is nothing to look at.
My bare feet curl to meet the surface of each stone.
The fog breathes and I breathe with it, until
a solid flesh is reprieved; no lines stand between
skin and the invisible water, no definition, only
unmaking, the way the world dissolves sometimes,
when we cannot put our fingers on the true soul
of the mystery. For instance, creation.
What the water knows it will not tell.
What the pall teaches is only a dissolution of boundaries,
how night and fog can erase a world we comprehend,
rob our memory of well-traveled paths until
we cannot grasp origins, remember only
that it was always dark, then, in the beginning,
love came into the world, and with it, loneliness.

A Measure

It's unlucky to know you're happy;
it's unlucky to say you're happy.
Touch wood. Cross my fingers. Spit.
—Jean Rhys, *Voyage in the Dark*

It startles me: the intricacy of emotion,
the constant navigation, the willful amnesia.
Every morning and every night, my love,

I tell you I love you and leave you
something of myself. Every day
I go on to work and earn something back,

but these are never the same things;
there is never an equivalency, never a balance.
Once, when I was twenty-three, I believed

I had found the right man because
he lived in a loft and led such
a bohemian life. Every night we made love

in a bed braced at the edge of a balcony,
a mirror propped against the opposite wall
and he would watch us as we grappled.

Somehow, he managed to live
both inside and outside his body
at the same time. I didn't understand then

why he left. Today, I know a little more,
have forgiven a little more.
When I wake with you

or when I wake away from you
I still say *I love you* to your pillow,
to the dawn, to some part of the new day

between us. Always, there is an accounting,
a debt joyfully paid. Always, I awake
and hungry, give you something back.

Natalie Says

That spiders bring luck, and so I leave the web hanging
in the corner of my room. Mornings now, I wake
with my body covered in small red bites, feel tired and sore.
Natalie says it's the seasons changing, but I suspect otherwise.
No flies in my room, no gnats, but a spider filled and a price
to pay for such good fortune. Natalie says the autumn
ushers in her sadness, the urge to drink from sundown
to bedtime. On winter evenings, she calls sometimes,
speech slurred, and tells me the stories she told the day before
when she was sober. We both love stories. I grew up
listening to both kinds: those told once with sharp tongues,
those told again with tongues sloppy. This story is mine,
for instance: baby brother, son, lover, friend, all listening
to the chimes of ice in the glass, possessing a laughter
brittle with anger. Look, this need not concern you,
the luck of spiders, the autumn's dusk coming faster
and faster with its slurred vengeance. That is your story:
the one about the limits of care, compassion sucked dry
by too much need. Natalie says the world has taught itself
not to listen too closely, and I try to cooperate.
As the light dwindles tonight, the leaves in the street clatter,
one brown brittleness strikes another, and I cannot help
hearing; it is all just that loud.

For Liam, When He Grows Up

She told me she named him William, Liam for short, for the Gaelic in him,
and now I should know, at least in name, I would live.

She would see to my legacy and I let it pass, though I did not care
to see a child called after me after most of the brandings I have worn.

Some days I sing lullabies to those unborn, all of my sons and daughters,
and I wait for the things I do not want: those children, that family, a wife.

Some days I wonder if my mind will change and I let the thought through
as I search for that particular desire, the longing for a child, in a chest

that does not accommodate the need. And some days (most days) I just sit;
content to seek what my love will bear, what his love will create with mine,

and there is never a child here, not from our twin hands.
She carries Liam in her arms and that sweet flesh, the flaxen hair

and water-blue eyes speak for her. Now, she has found a new voice
and it will carry and comfort her through another seventy years.

By then, I will be dead. I give her my proxy to bear all of my children:
William and Billy and Willy and Bill, faggot and cocksucker,

homo and queer. I will her my legacy of names and hates
and she passes on the small memorials: in the searing laughter

of a growing child; in cards sent at Christmas to *Dear Uncle Bill,*
Dear funny uncle, I hope you are well.

Autumn Variations

I.

Tonight my work is done but I'd rather not go
down to the lake, watch the sunset burning red

with the fires consuming Washington and Canada.

I'd rather not sit on a bench and watch the men
in their lycra shorts jog by, try to store up

enough autumn heat to see me through
another hungry winter. The maples

are turning red, like the sun, like the sumacs.

II.

My mother reports her yard has become
a rest stop for monarchs migrating south;

she brushed against a tree yesterday
and was engulfed in a cloud of butterflies,

hundreds of fiery wings flashing orange
around her head, a riot of beauty.

III.

If I must burn things I burn them in autumn,
make fuel of the necessities I'll learn to live without;

the smoke from the fire twists, acrid on my tongue,

but the serenity of consummation remains,
the distillation of the lessons taught to us by fire.

Put more blankets on the bed tonight,
set the clock to ring though our morning will break

in darkness; they say winter has come.

Two

An Alchemy in the Bones

The first element is fire.
    The second, seed.
        The third, blood.
            The fourth, danger.
The fifth, desire.

My bones have grown mouths,
    have grown paths,
        have grown rivers
            of lead transformed,

and I am coursed through
    with a better, killing blood,
and my bones are singing
    their songs of lives lived in flames.

Teach me to wear fire.
Teach me to transmute
    every stinging cell until
        I am covered in flowers.

Sleep

I count stars on the ceiling
long after he extinguishes the light.

I count stars on his sweet back,
naming each constellation of freckles

which dots the arch of his straight spine,
the scalp of his shoulders.

And always after he drifts to sleep,
I count the minutes out

on my curled hands and wait,
contented, but do not find rest.

I cannot sleep in his company:

in the risings of his chest,
in the singing of his sleeping breath;

I pull at his arm and draw him from the dark.
Then, he traces letters with his fingertips

on the pale skin of my abdomen,
sends blades slivering

through my stomach as I laugh,
and watch my skin,

his words there etched
in furrows I cannot erase.

36

Savoring Mangoes

He told me about a trip to Rio de Janeiro,
the concrete Christ with his arms spread wide
to welcome all but the pagans and the Jews.

There, he ate mangoes picked from the hotel trees,
sliced, drowned in thick syrup. The taste, he said, was sweet,
but pulled at him; when he realized he couldn't breathe,

he grasped at his throat and collapsed. The doctors spent
the morning prescribing and warning against allergic foods.
Last night in the restaurant I ordered chicken smothered

in mangoes—the crisp skin dyed yellow and orange,
the sweet that cuts the savory. The dish was nothing special;
I was raised in a northern world and have never developed

an appreciation for tropical life that moves beyond an awe
of things exotic. But he watched me eating
and in being watched I found myself rolling the mangoes

on my tongue, trying to show him some sense of unearned pleasure;
these were the lips which the fruit had passed,
which his lips would kiss when we were alone

and I wondered what fear might linger on lips,
of lips that had tasted what safety denied,
of lips that had savored poison.

37

A Torn Curtain

for Brett Klinker

The morning smells like cigarettes again;
the woman upstairs smokes
on the back porch and I wake
to a remembrance of your breath.
There isn't frost in California often,
nothing to obscure the long view
from a third-story window out onto
a skyline fronted by Duboce Park
and all of its dogshit.
Here, a tidal cold maps itself indifferently
across the frozen windows; I look out
at a face obscured by frost, flowing past
like the figure of someone glimpsed
through a torn curtain.
It is your face; it is the same face
passing down a hardwood hall
on the way to the kitchen
for morning potatoes and tobacco.
My senses make a book of memory
and I keep such a diligent catalog;
if you die now you leave behind
some record: a photograph
tacked loosely to a nail-eaten wall,
an empty pack of cigarettes,
the scent of spent matches and curry.

Mnemonic

He was making a catalog of all the things
he could still see; the list was diminishing

with the new loss of every lighted cell.
Hanging directly across from his bed

was the photograph of a pretty young man
who looked more dangerously young

than he was. Every morning broke with it:
a soft focus down on the crown

of pale white hair; flawless, closed-eye face;
a torso hairless, small nippled;

the model rose in uncontained edges
from the black frame of the photograph.

On the last morning, on the day the sun
disappeared and he would no longer distinguish

between daylight and fire, the photograph
would be there, the boy on his wall

like a still, enshrined lover burned
into the memory of an unreceptive lens.

This is all he wanted: a list of what his eyes
would no longer decipher, a memory of what

fingers alone would now have to read
from a small, dark catalog of beauty.

Notes for a Sacred Music

He says nothing
He says open a window
 the room is hot
 the blanket hangs
 across his shoulders
 like a single, damp wing
He says he is punishing me
He says the light you see
 at the end, the one
 we've talked about
 is nothing
He says go
He says nothing
He says no one gets sick
 unless they want to
 he wants to
He says go
He says the water is enough
He says the sky
 is not so raw today
 open a window
 the heat slips out
 the furniture heaves
 the room is pulled
 toward the casing
 as if some great sky man
 has finally drawn breath

He says go
He says it's rude to watch
He says the water is too much
He says it's like swimming
   a river you can only see
   you can't feel it
   you don't notice you're drowning
He says go
   it's rude to watch
He says shut the blinds
He says the sky is hungry
He says go
   leave the window open
   let the blind suck
   in and out
He says the sky is breathing
He says go
   he thinks he's sure this time
He says go
   he'll test the window
He says go
He says go
He says nothing
He says go

41

Cost of Living

I know he's been in the bathroom again,
left the light burning all night long,
like the limb of some illuminated tree
extending a single branch out to him
in the darkness. And maybe it was nothing,
just the dregs of dinner or too much water
at bedtime; there never used to be this paranoia
about the toilet. He is inconsolable in his
other bed, says fevers keep him flying away,
nightsweats keep him mean.
Sometimes, he sleeps in the bathroom.
I switch off the bulb on my way to the kitchen,
where he sits, drooping over crumpled news.
Not even in the morning can I be angry, not even
when he wrecks my paper, spills coffee.
I pull rumpled sheets from his hands, lay out
the comfort of ritual news. The mailman
drops packets through the door; the bills
have come today: phone, gas, electric.
Everything must be tallied new, expensive now
as medication and electricity make over our lives.
And he smiles, tired, as I add up the costs, wave
desperate debts in his face, and beg
Can't you put out the light?
Can't you just put out the light?

This Is a Test.
This Is Only a Test.

A flash of green at the base of the white wall. "Triton Moon" it's called, just enough black mixed in, no yellow. We are going to paint, but need to live with the color for a day or two, something small, a swatch, just to make sure it doesn't clash with the furniture because who needs more discord these days? Who doesn't get enough of it from the newspapers? The television? Last week I went to a clinic downtown, the anonymous one where you make up a name and number for yourself and come back to get your results at some preordained time. They drew a vial of blood from my arm and I called it 5-28-25: the date of my mother's birth, and the irony wasn't wasted on me, the knowledge that, if I flunked this test, the results would kill both of us. The sun just now across the wall. I follow the light as it moves from white to green, and crouch down on all fours to examine the effect. As I bend my arm, a slight pain in the tender flesh of the inside of the elbow, where the needle went in. Now it's nothing more than a small red spot, and by next week, when I get the results, the red will be gone. But not the green. The color in sunlight is ravishing, startling, as if something underground has been uncovered, and in the sunlight, allowed to spring into life. By next week it will have spread, with roller and drop cloth, brush and tape. Will have spread all across the walls of this room.

Constellations

Today I'm too tired to get out of bed. Instinctively I grope my groin, my neck, under my arms. I seek mounds of raised flesh mined, tender, dull, stinging. And always I remember: Today could be the first day of the end of my life. I count constellations: Big Dipper, Small Dipper, Orion's Belt. I flunked astronomy and hated science in high school, though now I take a more active interest in some aspects of the medical profession. I count stars: one dozen, two hundred, three thousand, until my reading eyes ache. And always I remember, numbers are relevant; but one or one hundred or more than one thousand (I know people who have passed that portion alone with partners they cannot name) the numbers are nothing. This morning, one is as good as one thousand; one thousand just means more experience below my belt, a better chance of having slept with a celebrity or somebody else's husband. Today I'm too tired to get out of bed. I run numbers through my head, count on the fingers of one hand my own paltry list of partners. And who could it be? If any have left a lasting impression in my scorched blood. Whose kiss, whose cock may have blessed me with a lethargy of dreams from which I will not awake? Hands steal down instinctively to my groin, to gain some darker proof for my exhaustion, begin the delicate dissection of every inch of my lymph nodes. This territory, I have come to know too well these past ten years, this territory mined, so soft, so dangerous to the touch. But I touch. And today, nothing explodes. I count one, two, three lack of lumps, let my hands go to wander other territories. Today, the constellations do not bloom in my skin, do not pour poison from my singing blood in any pattern I can trace. Today, I am still alive; the stars are on my side.

Quiet

By evening, the light has gone out of his face.
Everyone has something of the night in them;

the brush of a silk cloth across the cheek;
the seamlessness of eyes and mouth at dusk.

Making a tender bed is difficult when tired.
Finding the right words to express a voicelessness

of inertia, the pain in his throat when too much
has already been said. He lies on top

of the comforter and wonders if the night will cool.
Sometimes he wakes in sweats from no

particular dream, but kicks the blankets away
and stays uncovered until he wakes shivering

in the morning. There must be something
to say before sleep, the same way the dying

are obliged to impart something of wisdom
to the living before they go, as if,

in the transitions, they have already been privy
to the secrets of heaven. He possesses great candor

at night. Though his eyes belie a longing for sleep,
he speaks with the lights out, never wanting

to stop talking; as if the words, though tired,
act as a line, tying him to those to whom he speaks,

braiding him to the world of the waking, the living.

It Takes Me

some sort of a
            rhythmia takes me whenever I try to write about you
words and rhythm are never enough some sort of a
                        rhythmia takes me
I fail to build the better stanza fail to catch the music of the action of the
phrase it takes me: sitting in the car on a field road necking like there isn't
skin enough or time in the dormitory stretching out a hand to brush your
thigh by accident and stuck up against the wall you lift me take me down
in the ditch with an axle broken walk five white miles in January it takes
me: watching you drive from the back seat seeing some girl get all over
you like a lip-sticked snake it takes me: bent on the coffee table fucked
from behind like a cow mounted I whine and the wood's crisp edge
pressed a deep crease in the skin of my stomach some sort of a
                        rhythmia
takes me trick memory tripping
        out
            of sequence it takes me ten years practice a
                        rhythmia trampled I
learn to balance I quietly back down and you join the faces who fare no
better than a photograph left in the sun my elephant's memory stretches
out to meet you I catalog everything everyone and then you die and how
can I draw a poem out of dissonance how can I cut a poem from something
that has no clean
            breaks?
it takes me you die no poetry there no metrics and some sort of a
                        rhythmia
takes me some sort of halting cry of mourning done once and left to die
you can't be buried twice but you you treat me to repetition live again

46

screaming in the trees and some sort of a

                                         rhythmia takes me some
treacherous kiss some cock some carnal coward who left me at nineteen
stripped and crying you trip me John for a decade you trick me every
time I pull my pants down let's admit it I never knew you knew only the
bones you wanted revealed never dug beneath the flesh never happened
to find any discrepancies in the seams of your skin in the fit of your
clothes or your cock I cannot deny that stifling eye or the skill of your
pleasured body but what fit in the bedroom never worked on the bus on
the street with public life lived away from cum-stained sheets or words of
love what made sense in the bedroom never makes sense now in the
funeral pyre some sort of a

                              rhythmia takes me every time I try to translate
you to paper to poetry I've lost your language you will not make metrics
for me now not even in your grave.

47

Now That We Are Never Finished Mourning

for Mark Miller

Don't even start. It would be a long, ugly list.
How one morning Mark couldn't wake up and we recall
his wondering aloud whether he might turn into ashes
in Wisconsin. How his remains were flown home
in a plastic jar, back to San Francisco, not the Midwest,
because Wisconsin (or Minnesota, or the Dakotas,
or Michigan, or Iowa . . .) is a place which, once left,
can never be convincingly returned to again.
How Brett took the ashes to the Detour
and dumped some on the floor, bits of bones
and fine gray powder ground under the heels
of well-worn leather boots. It was all accomplished
in darkness. Other ashes scattered in the park,
under the stands of rhododendron, used condoms,
cigarettes, old gum, and Mark, seeping down into
the city's unstable soil. Don't even start.
I don't know enough stories, or maybe only
beginnings, or ends; say, the details: the translucence
of a man's skin in the afternoon light, a bit
about his hair or his eyes. Their names can be
alphabetized, but never ordered; I can never
do justice to them, their capacity for knowing
each exact moment, each heated contact,
the taste, the scent, the texture of skin.
Don't even start. I could say it all again,
retell every story I've ever told and still
no one would listen. Why should they?

Aren't we all tired of death? It used to be
we'd tell a story and something, some lesson
or knowledge, would be made or unmade.
And something else would change. Now, nothing.
Now that we are never finished mourning,
the shapes, the intentions of the stories have changed
and we all walk away, uninterested or weary
or used up when we read the obituaries
or hear one more poet on the stage proclaim
This poem is dedicated to the memory of . . .

A Widow's Song

for J

Your body says this. The thin hair on your head says this.
The varicose veins in your legs say this. Your skinny limbs,

the brown spots on your arms.
In Nepal, a little girl is given the nut from a bellfruit tree

and married to a Hindu god so she will never be a widow,
never sleep in the thin embrace of remembrance.

If you should die, where is the place that I will call home?
It has taken me too long to believe in refuge,

to trust the sincerity of need and ardor.
If I sleep in your arms, let your arms be a promise;

my breath weaves a rope that pulls around us, binds us.
There was never a ceremony when I was a boy,

no promises made to a spirit that I would never be alone;
when I am old, be old with me.

Three

There Be Monsters Here

Driving Sunday and suddenly the countryside I grew up in
is unfamiliar, the path from my mother's house to my sister's
unclear. Pulling to the side of a rough gravel road,

I open the glove, get out a map. For every one of eighteen years
I spent in this rural county, for every year I've spent since
running away, returning home, I should know these roads,

all paths that lead out from the forest, into the meat-steamed kitchen
where my mother resides, my fertile sisters at her feet.
But ten years in a city of neat, square blocks and buses,

rows of identical houses I can tell apart through
subtle differences, this has destroyed my sense of north, south.
I can no longer name any tree; and this map, senseless, might come

from the bottom of a sea chest or the floor of a tomb.
I turn it around and around like the wing of a windmill,
hope it will name a direction. I'm reminded of a class I took

as a freshman: Geography 101 and all of that history, those maps
the teacher held up from the Dark Ages and beyond, were fragile circles
stretched to encompass the whole world. But ancient cartographers

didn't have a large enough scope to complete their planet.
Trapped, they knew their own countries and the veiled regions
that bordered; and where there were places suspected to exist,

but uncharted, they drew fantastic creatures, cheeks puffed,
lips curled, blowing out the four winds and wrote
There be monsters here. In the yard of a farm across the road

53

I see three frayed children scrambling with an old tire, recall the smell
of hot summer rubber, the peeling texture of thin tread.
Those ragged strangers, aliens to me, scream at a dog, speak of everything

I have run so fast to forget. But with one last glance down the road
I am walking toward them, reminded of the fear of knowing,
of being left alone. The horizon sweeps up from gravel, vanishes

in the cloud of a passing pickup. So much dust to navigate
in the quiet country, so few farms like continents adrift in a sea
of wheat and corn. I call out ahead *Hello!* and wait for a reply.

The Window, Autumn

Outside, she rakes maple leaves into loose piles, stakes burlap and wire
around roses rarely coaxed to bloom. From inside, I watch my mother
through old windows as she is changed by the bend of the pane.

Old glass, slow as continents, drifts down over years,
pools at the bottom of the sill, and spreads the world out in a new spectrum.
Old glass, viscous as memory, runs unseen.

She moves on. The leaves sit in ordered mounds until the wind comes;
she begins to prune the hedges, collects grass at the base of the fence.
The summer starts to push away in the promise of a brittle breeze and

she cleans. She cleans. Outside, my mother is transformed,
a woman woven into the trees—her hands and face warped
and spread into the branches, a body bent and blending

across the lawn. Now, she knows a world without children,
lives in a place I've never seen. She stoops over, throws a stone
into the deep ditch, snaps down the brown milkweed.

Lobelia

for Ruth Gaube

The plants call for water
and the snails on their leaves
eat up a season's growth.

The neighbor children
on the patio below
are screaming, and their father,

his face sun red,
sits grinning;
something is always hungry.

The dahlia, she is told,
can grow blossoms bigger
than a woman's head,

and the lemon tree
buds now in a sweet, pungent scent
which reminds her of her mother,

the collection of ladies
gathered between the pews
of a Utah church.

Everything consumes.
Even she swallows
the meditative calm

of a well-appointed garden.
Even the lobelia,
a deeper shade of blue

standing stark against her skin,
resembling nothing born in daylight,
pulls her, greedy, to its blooms,

to their promise of
dark fragrance,
a finally sated night.

Jerry Lee Lewis Kills His Child Bride

On the backroads of Blue Earth County, I rode in the open back of a pickup
with my sisters, with three drunk brothers-in-law in the cab taking turns
pretending to steer. We called this joyriding, though my throat was filling
up with dirt, though my sister Linda sat propped against the cab, wheezing
through incomplete lungs, and the brothers-in-law kept opening up the
little window between inside and out and offering us beers. Jerry Lee Lewis
screamed out from the eight-track, caught in the loop of track two, over
and over again singing *Goodness gracious great balls of fire!* My sisters
discussed what they had just heard on the news: that this star who played
piano with his foot had been accused of killing his wife, the one he married
when she was thirteen. My sisters dreamed of this
and I dreamed too

white trash grand passion on the top
of a big black piano, of a man like Jerry Lee coming to lure us away from
the next kegger; the death, we let slip by; it was only an accusation. But I
wondered about pianos, and saw Mrs. Jerry Lee spread out in a pink chiffon
dress, her petticoats covering the whole surface of a piano-shaped swimming
pool; on this dry day it had to be a pool where she died, drowned with a
martini in her hand. The pickup plunged down a hill. We all screamed, and
Linda wheezed, looking like a skinny fish; death before celebrity would be
a shame. And it's really only a matter of degrees that separates the famous
white trash from the unfamous; any one of my sisters could achieve a beehive,
pink chiffon formal, crinoline bigger than her whole body. Our dreaming
father bought a piano one day, on credit, and promised us lessons.
In the summer.

But summer never came that year, and I
snuck lessons from a friend who said he wanted to be Vladimir Horowitz.
I said I hadn't heard his songs, and could he play the piano with his foot?

I managed *Für Elise* before the creditors closed in for nonpayment, and only managed to snatch my romance novels from the bench before they hauled the piano out the door. Our father said nothing. My sisters didn't notice. And I didn't care; the only time I really wanted to learn to play piano was when I watched the creditors carry the spinet down the steps, and load it into the back of their van.

Northern Light

Midnight and my mother walks
into the room where I sleep
with the television's blue glow.

She's just come off the evening shift
at the printing factory and small clots
of shaved paper cling to her clothes,

her ink-stained fingers.
She nudges me awake, her face
illuminated by the glowing end

of a cigarette. *Come outside* she says,
her eyes too animated for the late hour;
I obey, though I drag a blanket—

remnant of my sleep—behind me.
Late autumn cuts into my feet
as I walk onto the cement steps

and my mother points into the air
where the sky is alive with fire.
Color braids up in a wild cone

undulating, and light spills red,
green, blue, white
into the unaccustomed night.

Northern lights my mother says
and I am amazed as the factory drains
a little from her face, and I realize,

at this hour, in this strange light,
that it is almost possible
to believe in anything.

September Wedding
Fort Barry, California

Somewhere, I remember this train of linen, silk, wool, and cotton
moving, laughing down a hillside, toward a priest who waits

in the trees to wed one inexperience to another.
A clarinet plays, echoes against the branches of this cup of land

until I believe the musician is standing just behind me.
And a priest waits in the trees. And the sea is still cresting,

despite the bride in her long brocade, her protesting train
sweeping green into the water, as if, for all of us,

that was ever enough. Deep in my body, I remember this:
how we all marched out one day into the trees, how the sun

and the summer depended on what words were spoken,
how they were said, and to whom. From my porch view,

I shiver as this long, formal train twists through the meadow
below, and somewhere in my forgetful bones, I am singing.

Fort Collins, Colorado

She has three appointments this morning alone with the dean's wife, the doctor, the man at the museum. Then the luncheon, the banquet, the faculty wives. Member of every social committee, she streams down the streets of her suburbia, station wagon well in hand, makes lists on a notepad pinned to the dashboard, stamps letters with a dry tongue, and catches *fuchsia, lavender, white* blossom petals lining the streets in orderly rows; she steals a glance, makes a note to notice them before the end of the season. A truck rounds the corner; she's driving behind, and it's too sharp, too fast; truck wheels leave the ground; she locks brakes, drops pencil, stops making the list; she turns sideways, the truck sways nearly over and then back again to four wheels. She sits horizontal, spanning the road. The truck pushes on, unconcerned, only brushed the trees on the corner lawn and she feels them, the branches shaking, something vibrating up through earth and asphalt.

This is no time for moving.

She clutches her pencil, points to the list and watches it snow; May, and it is snowing. *Fuchsia, lavender, white* she writes fast enough to capture the color of every flake. She writes *fuchsia, lavender, white* and the windows are down, the snow comes in and it is so warm for the season, so late for snow. She writes *fuchsia, lavender, white* until the pencil fades from her hand, the dashboard drops away and there is only pure color left before her eyes, drifting down through the sunroof, blowing in from the driver's side. She knows she should be cold. She knows about weather, but she has never seen this snow before, shaking from branches, her own storm. She sits, drops pencil, tips head back and lets it all come down *fuchsia, lavender, white.* Her arms are covered in petals, her lap full, her head crowned in *fuchsia, lavender, white.*

This is no time for moving.

A House Over There

for Jeannette

She recognizes the carpet
with the stain by the door,
the slow odor of wet animals;

every house they live in
is the same.
What he hasn't pawned

she can carry in her purse: tickets left
for the television, the phonograph,
every instrument of pleasure

which he does not carry
on his body.
New dishes won't buy it,

a new couch leased
for too much interest,
planting flowers for a season

that she won't live out
in that particular house;
always, there is an air

of transition, and the chairs
that aren't thrown over in anger
jump about like nervous children

falling in the anticipation
of one more blow;
everything wants out of the way,

wants to be moving down
the darkening road,
on to the next site of contrition.

He Will Not Eat Rice

for Dennis

He will not eat rice
with butter, with chicken, with cheese,
not even with chocolate,
the way our mother makes it
like custard, chilled, in hot summer.
He will not eat rice
because it smells of jungles,
of steam rising sweet and sticky
from the barrel of a discharged gun,
because it smells of monkeys
hanging by tails, biting in play
until some soldier takes them,
one by one, crucifies them screaming
on the rippling walls of a corrugated tin shack.
He will not eat rice
because he's seen children picking
through shattered layers of villages,
dislodging every stone to turn up
some hint of food, of home.
Because he's seen what they eat,
when night sweeps away details;
under carbide flash their faces,
biting down into pieces of
rotting raw chicken, all of the maggots
like so many grains of writhing rice.
He will not eat rice
because it sours the taste
of beer and tobacco,
because it sticks on his fingers

66

when he eats with his hands
like the monkeys Christ-screaming
from the walls of the mess hall,
from the sides of his bed.
He will not eat rice
because it cleaves to his palate
as he struggles to breathe
through terminal smoke, and rain falls
through thick palm trees blown ragged
by every skinning blast,
because it smells of the mud
he wears like a mask as
he crawls through the trench.
He will not eat rice;
it reminds him of something
he will not remember but never
forgets: the look on the face
of the man down the barrel,
who took all the bullets,
who lost his poor head as he drained
down into the grave;
the one who ate rice.

Taking Pictures of the Moon

for Pinky Bass

Winter dreams of you as you dream of summer,
on the humid Gulf, dream of dry land, laying sheets

of unexposed photographic paper out across
arid Mexican ground, waiting in the night

for the paper to drink in an image of the pale moon
like a thin membrane of sand made moist at the sight

of the tidal globe. Save everything. The camera hangs
from your neck like a jewel; you collect whatever you pass,

a habit instilled by necessity, a need unmet in the past.
Now, nothing goes by that is not recognized,

and the hunger has migrated from stomach to hands
to eyes; whatever must be fed resigns itself to paper,

a slow progress of image as you drop the sheets
into the chemicals, rock the tray back and forth,

wait for the moment the moon appears, subtle and gray,
reflecting up from the rippled surface of the water.

Diane

My sister, a house haunted to the bone, has built herself again upon
the foundations of fire, where fire kissed her, where fire killed

her husband and three children. She paints the rooms of her new house
every day, starts in the basement, glowing white, and by the time

the attic is through, she can smell it again, just under the odor of enamel:
a subtle drift of smoke. She rubs burned fingers; she will forget.

She takes a new husband. They hang pictures over cracks in fresh walls,
set potted plants under windows as glass falls from casings, place buckets under

every delicate leak. She collects a new identity: stuffed animals inhabit
each empty room, and the kitchen is a flock of gingham geese flying toward home.

But the plaster cracks at the base, beams sag, and every night, cabinet doors
in the kitchen throw themselves open as one more wall settles into

burned, remembering soil; and my sister lies in her new marriage bed,
listens to her house sing, her hands clasped tight over memory's unwilling ears.

My Mother Visits the Site of the Fire

After the fire, nothing was left
but the stairs, rising withered
and black against January's
bitter sky.
      My mother fell
to her knees when she saw them.

This was the way
she always believed
visions might come to her:
      a sudden, vicious blow
to her chest, a visit
from God like a punishment.

Even after her legs
grew numb, she wouldn't leave
the stairs behind.
      God's stairs.
The stairs she remembered
from the Bible,
the stairs the angels walked down
when they visited Jacob
      in the dream.

Notes for a History of Someone Else's Grandmother

A bottle of aspirin mixed with some pills that have no name,
but stand in stark contrast: purple to white, red to white, yellow.

Take one color every four hours. Take one nap, wake,
make a phone call and collect up all of the photographs

taken in childhood. Hide them. The light in the mind
will diminish; the pictures, the letters will work to remind,

to remember, the limbs of a truncated history. Take one pill
every two hours and call someone in the morning,

the afternoon being reserved for correspondence.
Write this down: Your name, your age, your preference for dinner.

Nowhere is the water more poisoned. Nowhere do the thieves
of history prowl more successfully than here in this apartment.

They take every letter she has received, even the note
with the signature of the Kaiser, even the postcard

hand-colored in the Forbidden City. Take one pill every hour;
choose your favorite color. Nothing can go wrong.

All of the doors lock. The food is laid by and even winter
might arrive—she has waited for seventy years for snow—

even an earthquake. Some things will always remain buried
once the rubble has been swept up. Some things are kept from us,

71

even when discovered. Cover the letters with a silk kerchief
and hide them in the refrigerator, in the kitchen;

no one who is hungry will want them; no one who is hungry
will bother to notice a cloth concealing a sheaf of yellowed papers.

My Father Speaks

After he had been dead eight years, I couldn't remember
the sound of his voice, the tenor, the pitch, the Iowa inflection.
Maybe I never knew what he sounded like,

all of the years he was living, but moving away from me,
becoming memory before his body died. There is always
one price for forgetting, another for remembering;

the sound of his voice rides on the back of a memory
of his face, his hands large, fingers clicking together like sticks;
the dead, unrestful, unbury themselves

when we think too long on them, our thoughts
like a thin rope down into the earth, their pale hands
pulling up and up into an unaccustomed light.

A voice just now, through the window well;
a voice from the backyard, a voice from the trees.
It reminds me of someone. I cannot see who is speaking.

Three Funeral Songs for Linda

I. The Phone Call

I am sitting drinking coffee feeling morning
when she calls to say she has seen them again;

the dead do come home to roost above her bed,
our burned brother, his three children, all to say

they are waiting. She tells me this and asks me
to come and cut her hair. Make it short like mine,

she says; she doesn't have the energy to care
for the length of beauty now and do I remember

when we were children, and strangers mistook us
for twins? It will be that way again, she says,

but only for a time. She tells me she is dying.
Will I come and cut her hair?

II. Run, Letter

Tomorrow I will write her on a scrap of paper,
spelling out her name in careful letters.

My sister is a line on a page, a swing of ink,
a single dot. A script of ashes and a flat headstone;

my pen carves granite letters to spell her sign,
scratches five symbols to reconstruct a body

74

made of bone, draped in sallow skin and two eyes,
bigger than her whole head, brighter than stars.

My pen carves out her body as she lies in the bed,
in the funeral parlor, in the fire, in the ground

with her urn for an inkwell. I spell her out carefully,
no mistakes. I recognize those familiar shapes,

the line of the L as she sits up in bed, a stacked
cage of ribs, lips that bleed for water.

III. Anniversary

What the room tells in dusk are stories about rocking chairs,
blond bedroom suites, cedar chests.

What the room says is something about dust, the way dust
shudders in that last ray of daylight, swims across the room.

What the floorboards sing is a music of teenage footsteps passing
back and forth in front of the window, my sister Linda waiting

at night for the lights of a boy's car to press against the darkness,
drive her away with radio and lust, hands sliding inside thin cloth.

What the bed tells in the braille weave of a chenille spread
are stories of feet fanning beyond the edge of the mattress,

souls stretching beyond the length of the walls.
And the bed tells about waste: Linda's lungs grown thick

with mucus, pancreas, gall bladder ruined.
About thirty years too young to turn into a woman who tells me

I am dying every night in my dreams. I know there's always
someone here. The room tells me every time I return

to our mother's house, every time I open that door and go
into the room where nobody sleeps anymore.

What the room tells in dusk are stories of pillows and bed
left with an intricate impression, where weight was lifted

nine years ago and still, the mattress sags, the pillow
flattens and remembers where no head rests.

Still, the streams of light break across the floor and show
no footprints on the boards, no oval fingerprints on

the bureau or the tarnished silver brush. Dust settles everywhere.
And memory. Even on those in motion.

In the Lobby of the Hotel Saint Francis, San Francisco

Her gown, yellow-gold, fades in the afternoon light.
A debutante come to rest in the brocaded safety
of the hotel lobby, waiting, perhaps, for her party
to begin, waiting to be brought out, and thus, in,
to the arms of an eager, generous world.
Those who know enough to know are already
seeking her, their cameras offered like chests
filled with treasure for this newest, freshest goddess.
In the morning, the papers will be full of it:
Everyone who sat at her table. Everyone who
danced her dance. What they all wore.
The smartest of what the smartest said.
It will all be read with laconic grace by those
who could attend. With grave sincerity
by those who wanted to, but could not.
I can't recall her name at the moment.
I know I've seen her before, though
this new incarnation, newly emerging
in yellow and gold, has an adult's inclination
toward iciness. She sits in front of a window,
and outside, the raging garden coils in
upon itself, and the window frames the paths
and makes of them a study in contrasts:
A verdant painting, a canvas breathing
with the sunlight on her dress, the raucous red
of an amaryllis springing from a pot
behind her head. If I could say anything
I wanted at this moment, I'd probably sing.
The song would be quiet. No one would hear
the words. Just something brief, about blossoms,
their self-assured rapture, the secret
that is their serenity, in spring.

77

Time Lapse

On television, the documentation
of the formation of clouds and flowers,

an archerfish spitting a spear of water
at a fly, devouring it,

all in a matter of milliseconds,
captured on camera in slow motion;

the world is a diorama
for those who know how to watch.

The time I hit my lover,
for example. I am not a violent man;

yet, one hand ran out, ahead of thinking,
open palm, struck his face.

Or the time my mother cried,
trying to prepare potato salad

during menopause, could not find
the paprika, wanted only

my hand; I turned away.

Occasionally, I could use
that camera to slow the world,

to harness time, make it easier
to comprehend action, and inaction:

those fists, those kisses which
must be cataloged, dissected,

disengaged from heart's memory before
we can completely understand them,

if we ever can.

Unearthed

for Cynthia Stevens

Just say you are climbing stairs
and the moon is speaking
too loudly through old windows,
and you must stop, learn the warp
and weave of a new physics,
where light is refracted differently,
where sight and sound fuse,
and you, on your practical way,
must listen to the words
the lunar light speaks,
vibrating through bowed glass,
in a language you recognize
but cannot comprehend.

Photo by Laura Migliorino

William Reichard was born in 1963 and grew up in Smith's Mill, a farming village in south-central Minnesota.

Reichard has published work in many journals, including *Chelsea, Spoon River Poetry Review,* the *Georgia Review,* and *Cimarron Review,* and in the anthologies *The Perimeter of Light, Reclaiming the Heartland, Queerly Classed,* and *Gents, Badboys, and Barbarians.* His novella *Harmony* won an *Evergreen Chronicles* National Novella Prize and was published in 1995. He has received grants and awards from the Jerome Foundation, the Loft, the Academy of American Poets, the AWP, and the Minnesota State Arts Board. He has served as a Mentor for the Loft's Gay, Lesbian, and Bisexual Inroads Series, and was a poetry editor for the *James White Review* for many years.

Reichard is a member of the adjunct faculty at the University of St. Thomas and the University of Minnesota. He holds a B.A. in film studies, an M.A. in creative writing, and a Ph.D. in English literature. He lives in Minneapolis.